My great-great-great-great-great-grandfather... Was A Warrior!
© 2002 text and illustrations, Siphano Picture Books
First published in the United Kingdom in 2002 by Siphano Picture Books Ltd.

Published in Canada by:
Lobster Press™
1620 Sherbrooke Street West, Suites C & D
Montréal, Québec   H3H 1C9
Tel. (514) 904-1100 • Fax (514) 904-1101 • www.lobsterpress.com

Publisher: Alison Fripp
Graphic Production: Tammy Desnoyers

Distributed in the United States by: Distributed in Canada by:
Publishers Group West   Raincoast Books
1700 Fourth Street   9050 Shaughnessey Street
Berkeley, CA 94710   Vancouver, BC V6P 6E5

First published in Great Britain in 2001 by Mammoth,
an imprint of Egmont Children's Books Limited, London

National Library of Canada Cataloguing in Publication

Francaviglia, Riccardo, 1975-
     My great-great-great-great-great-grandfather-- was a warrior! / Riccardo
Francaviglia, Margherita Sgarlata.

ISBN 1-894222-81-4

     I. Sgarlata, Margherita, 1976- II. Title.

PZ7.F8448My 2003   j823'.92   C2003-903808-4

Printed and bound in Hong Kong.

My great-great-great-great-great-great-grandfather...

...WAS A WARRIOR!

Riccardo Francaviglia - Margherita Sgarlata

ONE MORNING, I was brushing my teeth in front of the bathroom mirror. Suddenly, I caught sight of a dark figure behind me...
It was a giant carrying an ax, with a beard and a Viking helmet – and he was standing in my bathroom!

What would you do if
you were me? I opened
my mouth and howled,

Aaaahhh!

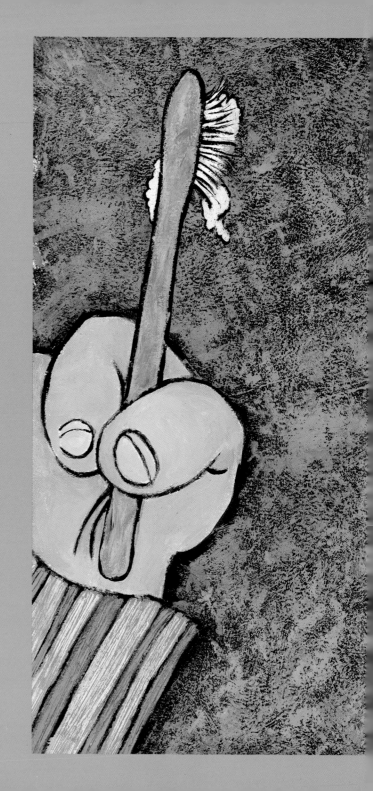

The man didn't notice how scared I was.
He lifted me up in his big hairy arms and said,
"Hi, Great-great-great-great-great-Grandson!"
"Wh-wh-who are you?" I mumbled.

"I'm your ancestor!" he said, "your great-great-great-great-great-grandfather."
"But why are you dressed like that?" I asked.
"I'm a warrior!" he said.
A warrior? I had an ancestor who was a warrior?

"What are you doing here?" I asked.
"I've come to meet you, G-g-g-g-great-Grandson," he replied.
"I want to see if you are at all like me."

Me – like him?

NO WAY!

My ancestor was going
to be very disappointed!

"G-g-g-g-great-Grandpa, are you a ghost?"
I asked. "Can other people see you?"

"Of course they can!" he said. "But look,
it's getting late – time for you to go to school,
and I'll go with you."

Go to school with him? What would my
friends say?

When we reached the school playground,
my friends asked, "Who's he?"
  "He's my ancestor," I said.
  "Your what?"
  "My ancestor."
  My friends began to laugh – and that's how
the fight started. Nobody teases my family and
gets away with it!

My great-great-great-great-great-grandfather just stood and watched.

"WOW!" he said, after it was over.
"You're a real fighter, just like me."

OH NO! Now I was behaving just like this ancestor of mine...

Then the bell rang and we went into class.

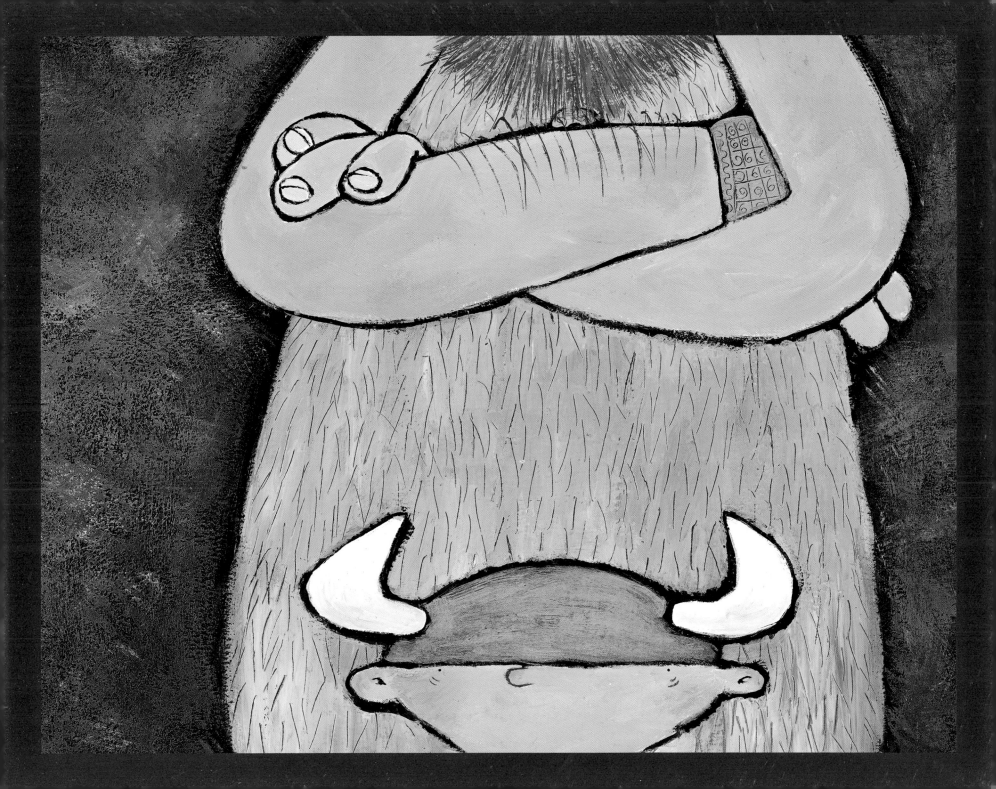

My teacher asked, "Mark, who is that man sitting next to you?"

"He's my ancestor," I said.

"Now, Mark, you're being silly, just because you don't want to do questions and answers this morning."

Then she asked me lots of questions about animals, especially cows and pigs. I got all the answers right and everybody clapped.

After school, my great-great-great-great-great-great-grandfather lifted me up and said, "Mark, I'm proud of you! All our tribe are great herdsmen – we know everything there is to know about animals."

As we walked home for lunch, I started to think, "Maybe I AM a bit like my ancestors... Maybe they weren't just big men with no brains!"

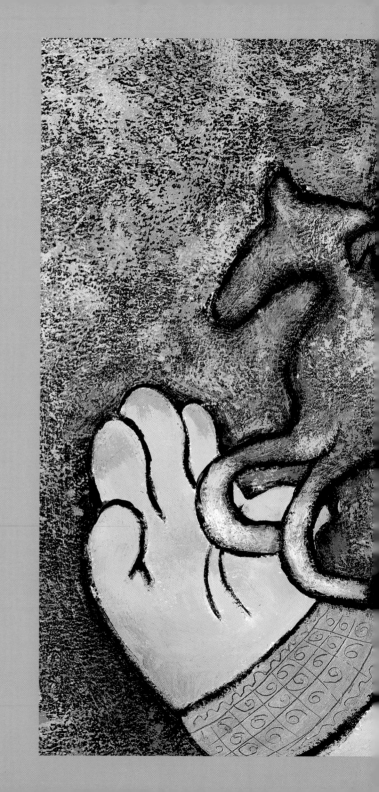

Back at home, I showed my great-great-great-great-great-grandfather my room. "What lovely pictures! So you're an artist like me!" he said, proudly pulling a painted stone out of his pocket.

Well, well! Who would have thought that my warrior ancestors were artists and drew pictures, just like we do? "I am just like G-g-g-g-great-Grandpa after all," I thought, "even if there are hundreds of years between him and me."

When at last we sat down to eat, I was hungry – but not nearly as hungry as my great-great-great-great-great-grandfather!

And watching him munch his way through plate after plate, I realized there was one big difference between us:

OUR APPETITES!